Victoria
the Violin
Fairy

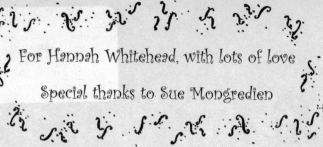

For Hannah Whitehead, with lots of love

Special thanks to Sue Mongredien

ISBN: 978-0-545-10629-0

12 11 10 9 8 7 6 5 4 3 2 1   10 11 12 13 14/0

Printed in the U.S.A.

First Scholastic Printing, January 2010

Victoria
the Violin
Fairy

by Daisy Meadows

LITTLE APPLE

SCHOLASTIC INC.

New York   Toronto   London   Auckland
Sydney   Mexico City   New Delhi   Hong Kong

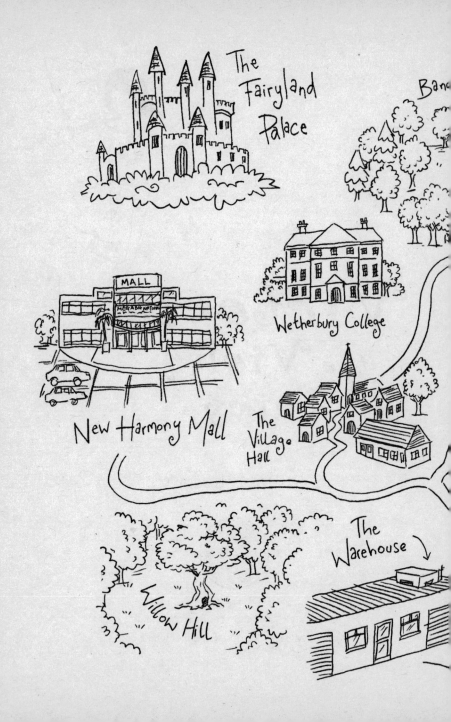

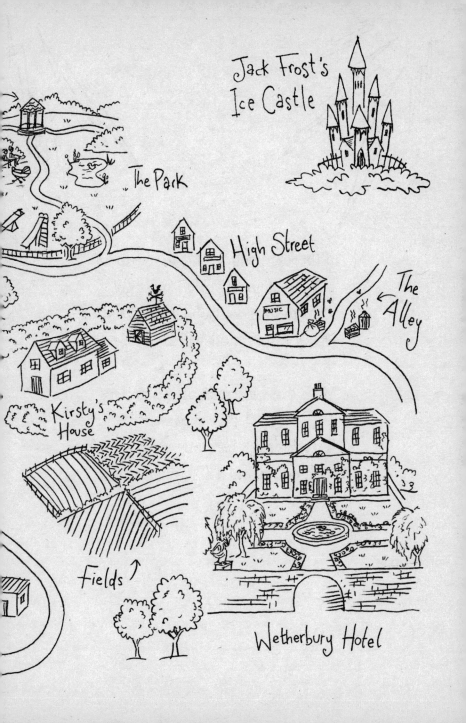

I'm through with frost, ice, and snow.
To the human world I must go!
I'll form my cool Gobolicious Band.
Magical instruments will lend a hand.

With these instruments, I'll go far.
Frosty Jack, a superstar.
I'll steal music's harmony and its fun.
Watch out, world, I'll be number one!

Contents

Listen to the Band

"I like that song," Rachel Walker said, pointing at the computer screen. She and her best friend, Kirsty Tate, were downloading music from the Internet, using a gift card that Kirsty had received for her birthday.

Kirsty nodded. "Me, too," she said,

clicking the mouse to download the song.
Rachel was staying with Kirsty's family
for a week over school break — and so
far, the girls had been having a very
exciting time! A very musical time,
too — helping the Music Fairies find
their lost magic instruments!
Mr. Tate, Kirsty's dad,
came into the
room at that
moment. "I was
just talking to my
friend Charles
on the phone," he
told the girls.
"Kirsty, do you
remember him? He
works at Wetherbury
College, and

he's been telling me about a really talented band that has been practicing there. He's sure they're going to do well in the National Talent Competition tomorrow."

Kirsty's ears perked up on hearing her dad's words. She and Rachel knew someone else who was determined to go far in the National Talent Competition — Jack Frost! He was so desperate to win the contest, he'd ordered his goblins to steal the Music Fairies' magic instruments. That way, his group, Frosty and his Gobolicious Band, would sound the best. Jack Frost wanted the first place prize — a recording contract with MegaBig Record Company — but Kirsty and Rachel knew that would be a disaster. Once the public discovered that Jack Frost wasn't human, all the girls' fairy friends would be in danger of being discovered by curious people everywhere!

"The band is rehearsing at the college," Mr. Tate went on, "and Charles asked if we'd like to go over and listen."

"Oh, yes," Kirsty said. "We'd love to!"

Mr. Tate nodded. "I'll drop you off there," he replied. "But I can't stay — I've got some errands to run."

Rachel smiled and got to her feet. "It'll be so cool if we get to see the winning band before the Talent Competition tomorrow," she said.

"And you never know," Kirsty murmured as Mr. Tate went to get his car keys, "we might spot another one of the magic musical instruments while we're there. . . ."

Rachel nodded. She and Kirsty had helped the Music Fairies find five of their missing instruments so far, but there were still two left to track down — the violin and the saxophone. The instruments were very important, because their fairy owners used them to make music fun and

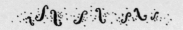

tuneful in Fairyland and throughout the human world. Since the instruments had gone missing, music just hadn't sounded the same.

Mr. Tate drove Kirsty and Rachel to Wetherbury College, and Charles let them in. "Bye, Dad," Kirsty said to Mr. Tate. "See you later!"

"Thanks, Charles," Mr. Tate said to his friend, then waved good-bye to Kirsty and Rachel. "Enjoy yourselves!" As Charles led the girls down a

hallway, his phone rang with a loud
ringtone.

Charles quickly took the call as they
walked along. Then he hung
up and pushed a door
open. "Here we
are — the
auditorium," he
said. "Let's go in."

Rachel and
Kirsty followed
Charles into a
large hall, which
had a wide stage
and rows of
seats. They could
see four figures on
the stage with their
instruments, rehearsing a song.

"Have a seat," Charles whispered. "You're welcome to stay for as long as you like! Just make sure you're quiet and don't disturb the band."

Kirsty and Rachel sat down at the back of the hall, and listened to the music. The band was playing a lively,

original tune that made Kirsty want to dance. "They're great!" she whispered to Rachel, tapping her feet.

"They have a really unique sound," Rachel agreed. "And they look so young!"

Kirsty gazed at the band members, who were far away on the stage. One was playing maracas, one had a banjo, another was playing a violin, and the fourth had a recorder. Rachel was right — the band didn't look much older than the girls themselves.

"How come those boys can play so well?" she said in awe. "That's amazing!"

Just then, a thought struck Rachel. The fairies had told the girls that the power of the magic musical instruments meant that whoever played them, or was close to them, was able to make perfect-sounding music. "I wonder if one of the magic instruments is nearby." Rachel whispered to Kirsty. "That could be why the band sounds so fabulous —

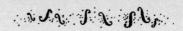

because the powerful fairy magic is helping them play!"

Then another thought hit her. "Kirsty — what if the band members are *goblins*?" she whispered in alarm.

Goblins on Stage

Kirsty leaned forward immediately to take a closer look. She and Rachel knew that Jack Frost had cast a spell over his goblins to make them blend in better with humans — so now the goblins were all the size of boys and were no longer green. The spell hadn't changed everything about the goblins, though. They still had big noses and large feet — and that was how Kirsty and Rachel had been able to see through their disguises so far.

The girls stared at the members of the band, but it was difficult to tell whether they were goblins or not.

The auditorium was very big, and Kirsty, Rachel, and Charles were sitting at the very back. "Charles, we're just going a little closer to the front," Kirsty whispered to him.

"Sure," he whispered back. "They're great, aren't they?"

"Really good," Kirsty agreed. Then she and Rachel tiptoed quietly up the aisle, heading toward the bottom of the stage so they could see the musicians better.

It wasn't long before both girls had no doubt.

With those noses and ears, the performers on stage were definitely goblins!

Kirsty and Rachel slid into seats near the front, ducking low as the band finished their song. They didn't want to be spotted by the goblins!

"That sounded great," the goblin on the banjo said. "I'm really getting the hang of this now. Not as good as when I had that magic guitar, of course, but still. . . . We sound amazing, guys. Jack Frost will be really happy the next time he hears us."

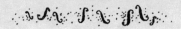

"When is Jack Frost going to be at one of our rehearsals?" the goblin on the maracas asked. "I know he thinks he's such a great singer that he doesn't need any practice, but I think it would be a good idea for us to rehearse together at least once or twice before the competition."

"You're right," the goblin on the recorder agreed. "But you know what the boss is like. He does things his own way. Come on, let's practice our next song."

As they listened to the goblins'

conversation, Kirsty and Rachel could hardly breathe from excitement. So this was Frosty's Gobolicious Band — without "Frosty" himself, of course!

"There are only two magic instruments left to find, right?" Kirsty whispered to Rachel as quietly as she could. The band started playing again. "Violin and saxophone. I'm pretty sure that violin up

there must be Victoria the Violin Fairy's
magic instrument, don't you think?"

Rachel nodded. "It must be," she
agreed, whispering right into Kirsty's ear
so that the goblins wouldn't hear her.
"But what can we do to get it back?
With Charles sitting back there listening,
we can't disturb the band. He'd be upset

with us — and then the goblins might get away."

Kirsty thought for a minute. Rachel was right — they couldn't make Charles suspicious by interrupting the rehearsal. But she and Rachel really needed to get the magic violin for Victoria!

As she was thinking, her gaze fell on the footlights at the front of the stage.

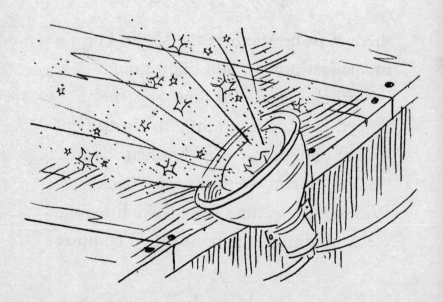

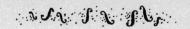

They were all shining a golden light on the band. But one of the lights was glowing with different colors, in a very magical kind of way. . . .

Kirsty nudged Rachel, suddenly hopeful. "Rachel, look at that multicolored light," she whispered. "I think it might be a fairy!"

Ring! Ring!

Kirsty and Rachel glanced at where
Charles was sitting. His eyes were shut
and he was leaning back in his seat, lost
in the music. "Let's investigate," Rachel
whispered.

The two friends carefully made their
way toward the footlights, hiding in the
shadows all the way.

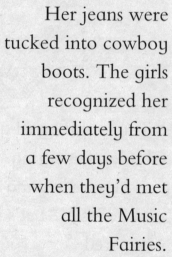

Suddenly, a small cloud of colorful
sparkles rose from the footlight, and a
tiny fairy appeared, listening to the music
with one hand cupped to her ear.

She had long, dark hair and wore a
pretty T-shirt decorated
with a butterfly pattern.
Her jeans were
tucked into cowboy
boots. The girls
recognized her
immediately from
a few days before
when they'd met
all the Music
Fairies.

"It's Victoria!" Kirsty murmured
happily, smiling in delight to see their
new fairy friend again.

The girls tiptoed up to Victoria. "Hi, there," Rachel whispered.

Victoria beamed when she saw Rachel. "Hello," she said in a silvery voice. "I'm so glad to see you. Those goblins have my violin, and I really need it back!"

Kirsty slid to the floor in front of the stage, where she'd be out of sight. She motioned for Rachel and Victoria to do the same. "Hi, Victoria," she said softly.

"We guessed that might be your violin — we recognized the goblins, and thought their playing was too good to be true!"

"The only thing is," Rachel added, "we'll have to get a man named Charles out of here before we try to trick the goblins. He's sitting at the back of the auditorium listening.

He told us we shouldn't disturb the band," she explained. Kirsty suddenly remembered how loud Charles's ringtone had been when he'd gotten a call earlier. "If he got a phone call, he'd have

to leave the room!" she said thoughtfully.
"I wonder if we could get his number
somehow and call him. . . ."

Victoria smiled. "Or I could
make his phone
ring with my
wand," she
suggested.
"And I'll use
some special
fairy magic to
make sure that
when Charles
answers his phone, there'll be someone
on the other end to keep him chatting
for a while!"

Rachel and Kirsty grinned. "Great!"
Rachel said. "Let's try it."

Victoria pointed her wand toward

where Charles was sitting, and gave it a few flicks. The air shimmered with magic, then Charles's ringtone echoed through the auditorium. He jumped up, patting his pockets frantically to find his phone. "Sorry — so sorry!" he called to the band, looking flustered and embarrassed. He immediately rushed out, the phone to his ear. The goblins stopped playing, and looked annoyed at the interruption. "Should we start that one again from the

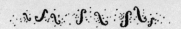

top?" the goblin with the maracas suggested.

The goblin with the violin shook his head. "I want to practice 'Goblin Serenade' now," he said.

"Not again!" the goblin with the recorder moaned. "We've already rehearsed that one tons of times!"

"He only wants to play that one because he has a long violin solo in the middle," the goblin with the banjo said sourly.

"That's why I need to practice it, banjo-brain!" argued the violinist.

While the goblins bickered, Rachel, Kirsty, and Victoria whispered about what to do next. "We'll have a better chance of getting the magic violin if we can separate the goblin with the violin from the others," Rachel said. "Otherwise, we'll be outnumbered."

Kirsty had an idea. "What if we shine a light at the front of the stage?" she said slowly, thinking as she spoke. "If the violinist has a solo, he'll probably step into the spotlight. And when he does, we could lower one of the scenery backdrops behind him, cutting him off from his friends!"

Victoria grinned. "And when he's on his own, we can get my violin!" She laughed. "Kirsty, that's a wonderful idea!"

Rachel was smiling, too. "Great idea," she said, gazing at the side of the stage. "It looks like we can lower the backdrop by pulling on those ropes over there — do you see?"

"And I can turn on and aim the spotlight with my magic," Victoria added. "It's a perfect plan!"

The goblins had started playing another song by now, and the girls tiptoed to the side of the stage and hid in the folds of the curtain.

Victoria hovered above them. As soon as the goblin with the violin began 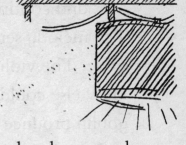 his solo, she waved her wand at the center spotlight above the stage. The spotlight swiveled, then turned itself on, shining a bright pool of light at the very front of the stage.

The goblin with the violin looked delighted, and walked forward to stand in the center of the light. He shut his

eyes and continued to play beautifully. The melody sent shivers down Kirsty's spine. The violin had to be very magical. How else could the lumpy-fingered goblin produce such incredible music?

"I think this is the rope, Kirsty," Rachel said just then, putting her hands on the thick brown cord that dangled from the top of the curtains. "If we both pull on it, we should be able to lower

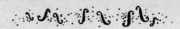

the scenery panel — and separate
the goblins."

Kirsty took hold of the rope, too, and
looked at Rachel. "Ready?" she
whispered. "One, two, three . . . PULL!"

Curtain Call!

The two friends held their breath as they yanked on the rope. Would their plan work?

"Yes!" cheered Rachel softly as the scenery panel slowly dropped down behind the violinist. Now he was completely cut off from his goblin friends.

The backdrop that hung behind the goblin showed a winter wonderland scene, with snowy mountain peaks and ice skaters on a frozen lake. The girls could hear the rest of the band shouting through the backdrop to their friend. "How did that happen? Are you all right, buddy?" they called.

The goblin playing the violin was so
wrapped up in his music, he didn't notice
their shouts. He just went on playing! He
shut his eyes as he
picked out the
melody.

"Charles might
be back anytime,"
Rachel remembered.
"Do you think we
should close the main
curtains, too? That
way, the goblin with
the violin will be
trapped between the curtains
and the scenery, and Charles won't be
able to see what's happening if he
walks in."

"Good idea," Victoria said, waving her wand. Red sparkles crackled from its tip, and glittery fairy magic streamed all over the heavy, velvety curtains. Moments later, the curtains had magically swung closed in front of the goblin.

Kirsty, Rachel, and Victoria went quietly onto the stage, being careful not to disturb the musician. "You'd better stay out of sight," Kirsty told Victoria.

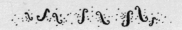

"We'll have a better chance of getting the violin if the goblin doesn't know you're with us."

"You're right," Victoria said, tucking herself into Kirsty's pocket. "I'll hide in here."

Just as her glittery wings vanished from view, the goblin stopped playing and opened his eyes. Then he blinked and stared around in confusion. Even with the light shining down on him, it was much darker on the stage now that the curtains were closed.

"Bravo!" Kirsty shouted loudly, trying to drown out the cries of the other goblins behind the backdrop. "Fantastic!" Rachel clapped as hard as she could. "That was wonderful," she agreed, stepping closer to the goblin.

The goblin bowed, but as he did, he noticed the snowy backdrop behind him and straightened up immediately. Looking puzzled, he shivered. "How did I get outside?" he wondered in confusion. "Are my friends hiding in the snow?"

"It's just scenery," Kirsty replied, thinking quickly. "You're not really outside. We're . . . we're the stagehands, you see. The scenery panel fell down by mistake. Sorry about that! I'll hold the violin for you while you go under it, if you want."

Rachel was impressed by her friend's quick wits, and backed her up at once. "Yes, your friends are right on the other side of this picture," she added. The violin-playing goblin looked from Kirsty to Rachel to the backdrop, still frowning. "Hey, you guys! Are you there?" he shouted. "I'll be there in a minute. Stay where you

are." Then he
looked down at
his violin and
clutched it a
little tighter. "I'll
hold on to this,
though," he told the
girls snobbily. "It's a
very valuable instrument, this violin
of mine."

"Hmnph!" sniffed Victoria from her
hiding place in Kirsty's pocket. Kirsty
guessed that she didn't like the way the
goblin had said that the violin belonged
to *him*.

Rachel pretended she was struggling to
raise the backdrop. "It's . . . very . . .
heavy," she panted, letting it fall again.
"We won't be able to lift it very high.

I'm afraid you're going to have to crawl on the floor to get under it."

The goblin looked appalled. "Crawl?" he echoed. "World-class musicians don't crawl, thank you very much! Don't you know who you're talking to? The future winner of the National Talent Competition, that's who!" He drew himself up to his full height, and puffed out his chest. "Besides, I can't crawl through there with my violin," he went on. "It might get scratched or damaged — and I can't let that happen."

"Well, that's why I offered to hold it for you," Kirsty said. "And then, once you're safely on the other side, I'll pass it to you. I promise I'll be careful."

The goblin considered this for a moment, but then shook his head. "No," he said, holding the violin protectively against his chest. "I can't risk it. I don't want anyone else touching my precious violin."

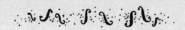

"*His* precious violin!" Victoria muttered angrily from Kirsty's pocket. Kirsty had to pretend to cough so that the goblin

wouldn't hear the fairy. The goblin edged slowly toward the backdrop. "I'm going to put my violin down on the floor, crawl under the scenery backward, then pick it up when I'm on the other side," he decided. Then he glared at the girls. "And you'd better not try any funny business," he added suspiciously. "I'll be keeping a close eye on you!"

Two Violins

"Of course," Rachel said politely, although her mind was whirling. How were they going to get the violin?

Then, out of the corner of her eye, she spotted a cardboard box full of instruments at the side of the stage. Someone had written WETHERBURY COLLEGE ORCHESTRA on the side of the box, and there, on the top, was a violin. Rachel's eyes grew wide with surprise the moment she saw it. What a stroke of luck! It gave her an idea that just might work. . . .

"Victoria," she whispered, moving closer to Kirsty so that she could get the little fairy's attention, "could you use your magic to turn out the lights when the goblin puts down his violin? We might be able to arrange a swap in the dark."

Victoria peeked over the edge of Kirsty's pocket. Her eyes brightened when she followed Rachel's gesture and saw the second violin. "No problem," Victoria whispered back, giving a thumbs-up sign. "Good thinking, Rachel!"

Kirsty grabbed ahold of the scenery backdrop and looked at the goblin. "Ready when you are," she said to him. Rachel, meanwhile, slipped over to the box of instruments and hid the ordinary violin behind her back.

The goblin put the magic violin on the floor and got down on

his hands and knees. Rachel took a step
closer to him, and he scowled. "You stay
there," he ordered her. "I don't trust
either of you!"

Rachel stopped obediently, and the
goblin began to crawl backward under
the backdrop. As soon as his head was
through, Victoria quickly waved her
wand — and the lights went out!

The stage plunged into darkness. "What's happening?" the goblin yelled furiously, but Rachel had no time to answer. Her heart pounding, she reached down to where the goblin had left the magic violin and grabbed it, skillfully exchanging it for the ordinary one. Quickly, she stepped away again — just as she heard the goblin reaching around

on the floor. "Here it is!" she heard him say, his voice muffled.

There was a faint clattering as he dragged the ordinary violin under the backdrop. "Ha!" the girls and Victoria heard him shout triumphantly. "You might have tried to trick me, turning off the lights like that, but I've still got my violin!"

"Oh, no he doesn't," Rachel whispered, stumbling through the darkness back to Kirsty and Victoria. "It's right here!" Victoria flicked on the lights

again with a wave of her wand, and
Kirsty, who'd been holding up the
scenery panel, let it drop
as she saw that the
goblin had vanished
on the other side.
Victoria clapped her
hands in delight at
the sight of her magic
violin in Rachel's hand.
"Wonderful!" she cheered, fluttering
over joyfully. "That worked perfectly,
girls!"

The sound of a goblin's voice came
through the backdrop loud and clear as
he spoke to his friends. "There were some
girls over there who were trying to trick
me into giving them the magic violin.

But don't worry!" he said. "I didn't fall for their silly tricks — I've still got it right here."

Then came the sound of violin-playing — a completely tuneless, scraping noise that made Victoria cover her ears. The music from the ordinary violin wasn't *awful* — it was still close enough to Victoria's magic violin to prevent that — but it didn't sound anything like the gorgeous, moving music the goblin had played earlier.

"That's not right," the girls heard him say, sounding confused. There was a long

pause, and then the truth dawned on him. "Hey! I *have* been tricked. Those girls stole my violin!"

"Let's get it back!" came a furious shout from another goblin. "Quick!"

The girls gasped as they saw goblin arms and legs appear under the backdrop. The goblin band was trying to scramble underneath the scenery!

Kirsty and Rachel both tugged at the velvet curtains at the front of the stage, trying to escape. But the material

was thick and hung in gathered folds, and neither of them could find the opening.

"Victoria, help!" Kirsty cried, full of panic. "We're going to be trapped!"

Fly Away!

Victoria tossed a handful of fairy dust over the girls, and they immediately shrank down to fairy size. So did the magic violin, which was still in Rachel's grasp. "Follow me," Victoria called out, quickly beating her wings so she flew straight up in the air.

Kirsty and Rachel copied her, zooming upward just as the goblins crawled under the backdrop, tumbling to the center of the stage.

Victoria waved her wand at the curtains, and they swung open just wide enough for the three fairy friends to fly through. Kirsty looked over her shoulder to see the curtains close themselves again. Then, lumps appeared in the material as the goblins tried to fight their way through to the front of the stage.

"This is all YOUR fault!" one yelled. "Why did you let those girls get the violin?"

"They tricked me — how was I supposed to know?" came the angry reply.

"Jack Frost will be furious when he hears about this!" a third goblin wailed. "Now we'll have to go back and break the news to him."

The curtains went still and there was some angry muttering, but Kirsty and Rachel couldn't make out the words. Then came the sound of the goblins stomping away, still bickering with one another.

The girls and Victoria held their breath for a few minutes, but the auditorium was silent.

"I think they're gone," Victoria said in relief. She led the girls to perch on one of the auditorium seats. Her eyes shone with happiness as Rachel handed over the magic violin. Blue sparkles flashed all around it, and Victoria smiled. "Thank you so much," she said gratefully. "Now that I have my violin again, music will sound even better throughout Fairyland and in your world." She rested the violin under her chin and played a few notes, and Kirsty and Rachel smiled in delight at the beautiful melody.

"I'd better turn you back to your normal size now," Victoria said, and waved her wand over them both. The air

was filled with
glittering fairy magic.
Kirsty and Rachel
found themselves
getting bigger and
bigger, until they
towered over
Victoria as girls again.

"I guess we'd better
keep an eye out for Charles,"
Kirsty said. "It's almost time for us to
go home."

"Let me just tidy up first," Victoria
said, pointing her wand at the stage
and mumbling some magic words.
The curtains swung open to reveal the
backdrop lifting back up to the roof of
the stage, and the ordinary violin flying
back to the instrument box. "There," she

said. "Thanks again. And please watch
for the magic saxophone. It's the only
instrument Jack Frost has now, so he'll be
guarding it closely."

"We'll be on the lookout," Rachel
promised. "Bye, Victoria. That was fun!"

"Bye, girls," the fairy said. "Now I'll
take my violin back to Fairyland where
it belongs!" With a flurry of violin music,
she disappeared.

Just then, the auditorium doors opened
and Charles came in. "What happened

to the band?" he asked,
seeing the empty stage.
Kirsty and Rachel
exchanged glances.
"They had to go,"
Rachel replied
truthfully.

"I was actually just talking to your dad on the phone," Charles said. "He's coming to pick you up."

"Thanks, Charles," Kirsty said. "I really enjoyed listening to the music."

The two friends went out to the parking lot to meet Mr. Tate. "I can't believe the National Talent Competition is tomorrow," Rachel said as they walked. "We have to find the magic saxophone as soon as possible."

Kirsty nodded. "We have to stop Jack Frost from winning the competition," she added. "I think we're in for another *fairy* busy day, Rachel!"

THE Music FAIRIES

Victoria the Violin Fairy's magic
instrument is safe and sound in
Fairyland! Can Rachel and Kirsty help

Sadie

the Saxophone Fairy

find the final missing instrument?

Join their next adventure in this special
sneak peak!

The Competition Begins

"We'd better hurry, Kirsty," Rachel
Walker said to her best friend, Kirsty
Tate, as they jumped out of the car.
"The talent competition will be
starting soon!"

The girls waved at Mrs. Tate, who had
just dropped them off. Then they hurried
into the New Harmony Mall.

"Good afternoon, everyone," said a voice over the loudspeaker system as the girls went inside. "The auditions for the National Talent Competition are about to start, so please make your way to the north end of the mall."

Rachel and Kirsty glanced at each other as they wove their way through the crowds.

"There are lots of people here, aren't there?" Kirsty said anxiously. "I hope we get Sadie's magic saxophone back before Frosty and his Gobolicious Band take the stage!"

The girls had been asked by their friends, the Music Fairies, to help them find their seven magic musical instruments, which had been stolen from Fairyland's Royal School of Music by

Jack Frost and his goblins. The magic musical instruments were extremely important because they made music joyful and harmonious for everyone in both the human and fairy worlds. Since the instruments had gone missing, music everywhere had been ruined.

Rachel and Kirsty had managed to return six of the magic instruments to Fairyland, but they were still looking for Sadie's saxophone, and the girls knew that time was running out.

"I'm *so* worried that Jack Frost and the goblins are going to win the competition," Rachel confided to Kirsty as they hurried toward the stage that had been set up at one end of the mall. "If Frosty and his Gobolicious Band win that recording contract with MegaBig

Records, it won't be long before *everyone* finds out about the existence of Fairyland!"

"I know," Kirsty agreed. "And even though Jack Frost only has one of the instruments left, its magic is so powerful that he could still win the competition!"

SPECIAL EDITION

Three Books in One!
More Rainbow Magic Fun!

■SCHOLASTIC
www.scholastic.com
www.rainbowmagiconline.com

HiT entertainment

RMSPECIAL2

There's Magic in Every Series!

The Rainbow Fairies

The Weather Fairies

The Jewel Fairies

The Pet Fairies

The Fun Day Fairies

The Petal Fairies

The Dance Fairies

Read them all!

📖 SCHOLASTIC

www.scholastic.com
www.rainbowmagiconline.com

HIT entertainment

RMFAI